D0604189

D0604189

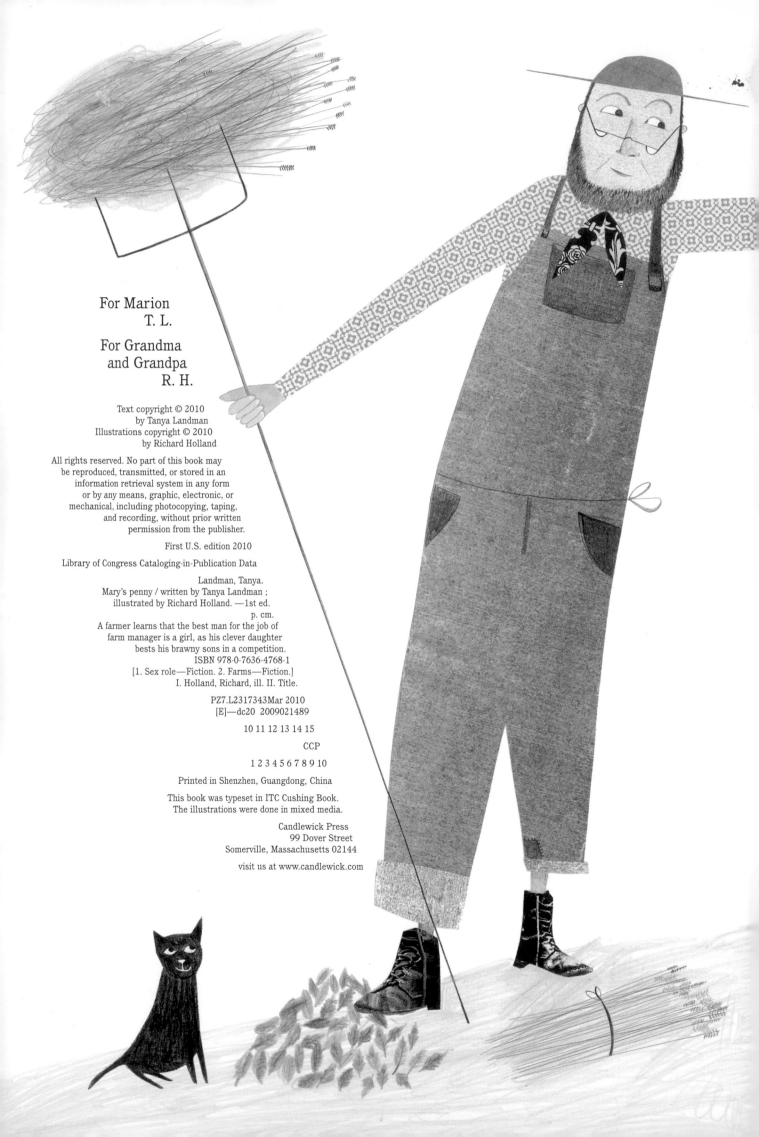

For Marion
T. L.

For Grandma
and Grandpa
R. H.

Text copyright © 2010
by Tanya Landman
Illustrations copyright © 2010
by Richard Holland

First U.S. edition 2010

Library of Congress Cataloging-in-Publication Data

Landman, Tanya.
Mary's penny / written by Tanya Landman ;
illustrated by Richard Holland. —1st ed.
p. cm.
A farmer learns that the best man for the job of
farm manager is a girl, as his clever daughter
bests his brawny sons in a competition.
ISBN 978-0-7636-4768-1
[1. Sex role—Fiction. 2. Farms—Fiction.]
I. Holland, Richard, ill. II. Title.

PZ7.L2317343Mar 2010
[E]—dc20 2009021489

10 11 12 13 14 15

CCP

1 2 3 4 5 6 7 8 9 10

Printed in Shenzhen, Guangdong, China

This book was typeset in ITC Cushing Book.
The illustrations were done in mixed media.

Candlewick Press
99 Dover Street
Somerville, Massachusetts 02144

visit us at www.candlewick.com

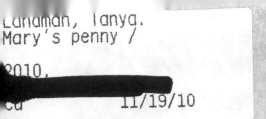

Mary's Penny

Tanya Landman

illustrated by

Richard Holland

CANDLEWICK PRESS

Long, long ago—

way back in the golden, olden days—

there lived a farmer

and his three grown-up children:

Franz, Hans, and Mary.

FRANZ

was brawny. His arms were as thick as branches,

and his hands were as big as stone slabs.

HANS

was beefy. His legs were as thick as tree trunks,

and his feet were the size of rowboats.

Then there was

Mary.

Mary was neither brawny

nor beefy. Her arms and legs

were as slender as sticks.

Mary didn't say much.

But Mary had a very special,

secret something:

Mary had brains.

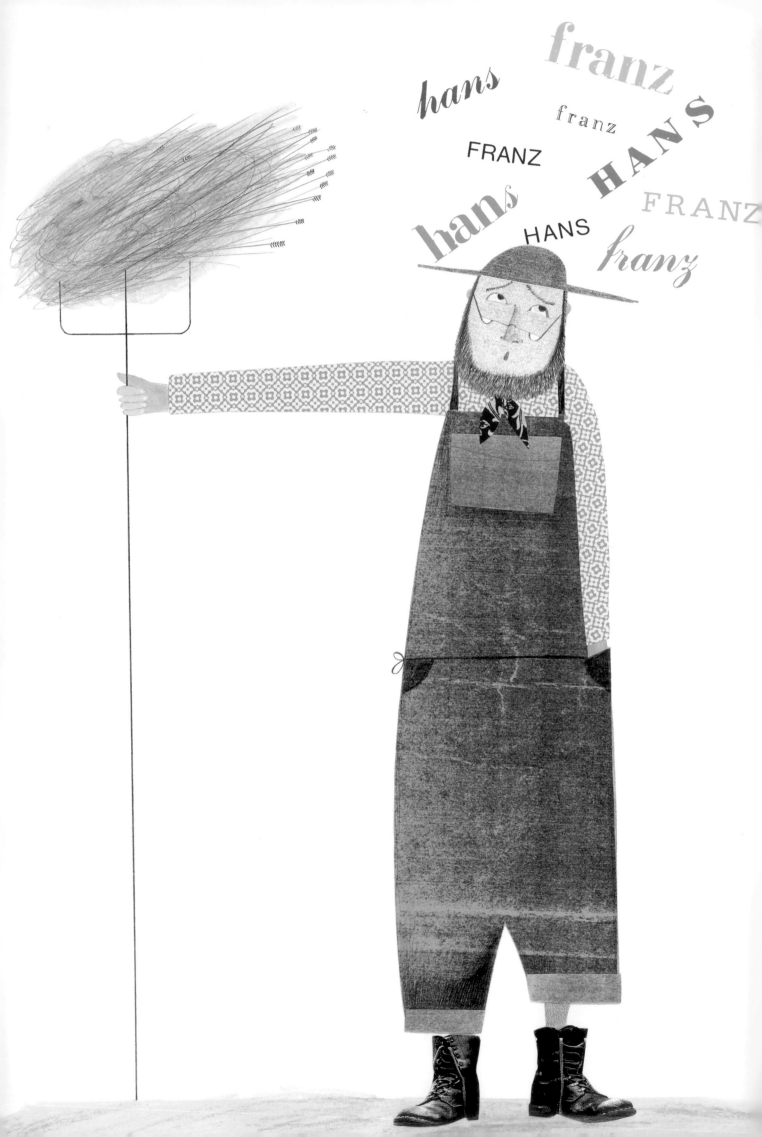

The farmer had a problem.

He simply couldn't decide who should run the farm

after he was dead and gone.

Should it be

FRANZ or HANS?

Should it be

HANS or FRANZ?

Franz or Hans? Hans or Franz?

All day long the names went around and around in

his head. It didn't occur to him to think of

Mary,

because this was long, long ago—

way back in the golden, olden days—

and everyone thought that girls couldn't

run farms.

One bright morning, the farmer called his sons to him.

"I have an idea," he said. "We'll have a competition.

Whoever wins the competition will run

the farm when I'm dead and gone."

The farmer dug deep into his pocket and pulled out

two bright pennies. He handed one to

FRANZ and one to HANS.

"With your one penny, you must each buy something

that will fill the whole house."

Franz and Hans scratched their

heads and tried to think.

Mary

watched and listened and

said nothing.

FRANZ

was the first to try, and the next morning,

he set off for the market. He looked at apples

and pears and milk and cheeses.

But in the end he bought a cartload of straw,

because this was long, long ago—

way back in the golden, olden days—

and you could buy an awful lot of straw

for a penny.

He piled it in the cart, up and up, until the cart

was so heavy that the horse could hardly pull it.

When

FRANZ

got home, he started to fill the house with straw.

He carried and stacked, and carried

and stacked, and carried and stacked,

and the house got fuller and fuller and fuller.

He covered the floor with straw, and then the pile

started to rise up the walls. He had gotten

halfway up the windows when he ran out.

There was no more straw left.

Franz had failed.

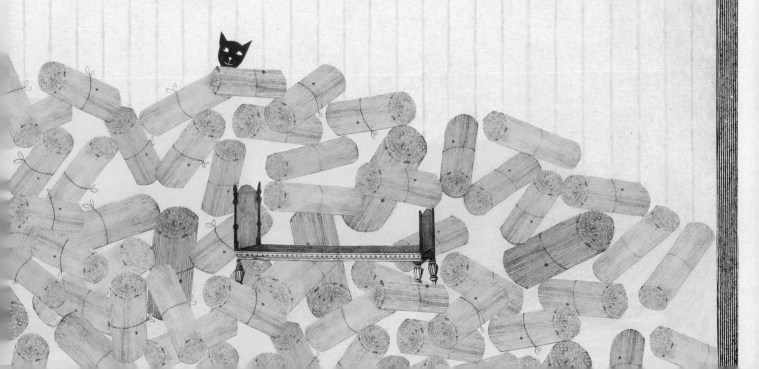

That night, they all had to sleep in the barn.

The next morning,

HANS

set off for the market. He looked at apples and

pears and milk and cheeses.

And in the end he bought a cartload of feathers,

because this was long, long ago—

way back in the golden, olden days—and you could

buy an awful lot of feathers for a penny.

He piled sacks in the cart, up and up, until

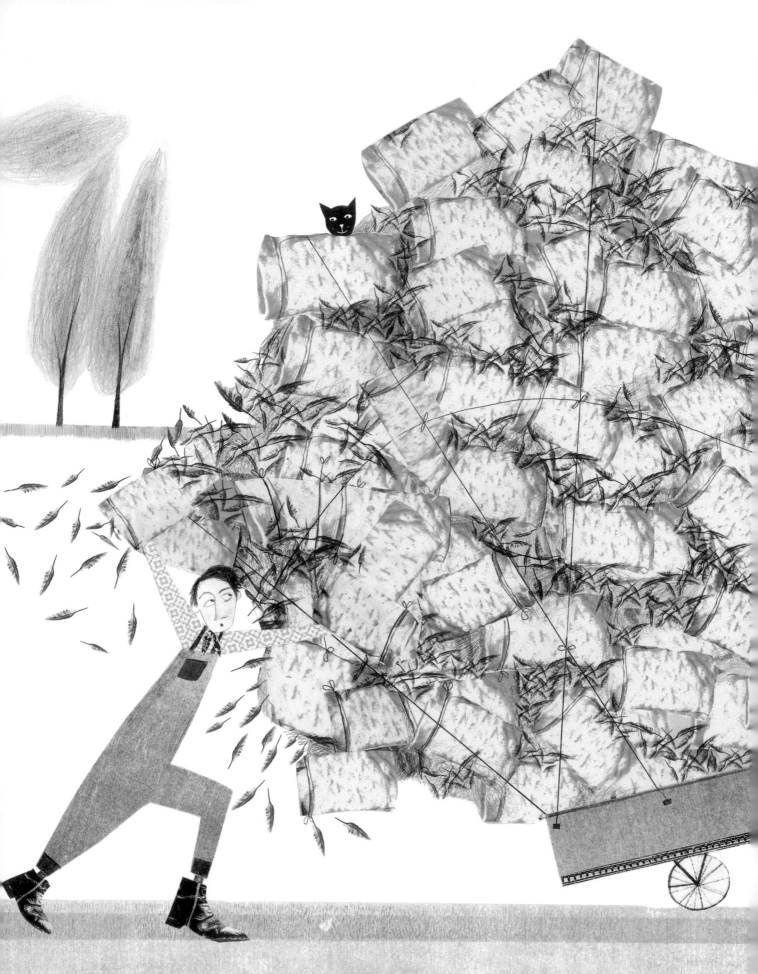

the cart was so heavy that the horse could hardly pull it.

When he got home, he started

to fill the house with feathers.

HANS

carried and stacked and sneezed,

and carried and stacked and sneezed,

and carried and stacked and sneezed,

and the house got fuller and fuller and fuller.

He covered the floor with feathers, and then the pile

started to rise up the walls, up over the windows, and

almost as high as the rafters. Almost. He had gotten

nearly all the way to the ceiling when he ran out.

There were no more feathers left.

Hans had failed.

That night, they all had to sleep

in the barn again.

"WHAT AM I TO DO?"

wailed the farmer sadly.

"WHAT AM I TO DO?

What am I to do?

What am I to do?"

Mary

watched and listened. Then she asked,

"Where's *my* penny?"

The farmer looked at her.

"You?" he spluttered. "But you're a *girl*!

Everyone knows that girls can't run farms."

"Father," said Mary quietly.

"It takes brains, not brawn, to run a farm.

Give me *my* penny, and I'll show you."

Slowly, reluctantly, the farmer dug deep in his pockets

and took out his very last penny.

Mary set off for the market. She did not look at apples

or pears or milk or cheeses. She did not look at straw or feathers.

Instead, she went straight to the candle maker and bought

a small candle and a tinderbox with which to light it.

This was long, long ago—way back in the

golden, olden days—and candles didn't cost much.

Mary had some change from her penny.

She visited the knife seller and bought a tiny penknife.

Then she went down to the riverbank,

cut a length of hollow reed,

and sat in the warm sunshine,

working at the reed with her little knife.

When the sun began to set,

she returned home.

It was dark when she called her father

and two brothers into the farmhouse.

Mary said nothing.

She struck the tinderbox and lit the candle.

She lifted the river reed to her lips and blew,

and out came the sweetest, softest melody.

When she had finished playing, there

was a very long silence.

At last the farmer took

Mary's hand in his and said quietly,

"Mary,

you have filled the house not once

but many times over. You have filled it with light,

and so filled it with knowledge.

You have filled it with music, and so filled it with joy.

And because you have filled the house with light

and knowledge and music and joy,

you have also filled the house with wisdom.

You shall run the farm from

this day forward."

And even though this was long, long ago—

way back in the golden, olden days—

when everyone thought that girls

couldn't run farms . . .

Mary did.

And the farm prospered

and flourished.